Jig-Saw Pieces

BOOK ONE

By

Violet Pilgrim

Published by New Generation Publishing in 2017

First Edition

www.newgeneration-publishing.com

New Generation Publishing

1

My life seems to have been one of jig-saw pieces which in the course of many long years have been made into a picture of what is perhaps going on behind the scenes of this world, and just in case I am meant to show it I shall try to do so, while I still can, being 94. I don't want to dolly it up for popular consumption nor to intrude into it much of my personal life or emotions as essentially I am pretty much the same as most people. Although some of this story, I must admit could be quite reasonably seen as preposterous. In respect of which I wish to state that I do understand this, that I appreciate the brilliance of modern psychiatry, and that I do try to always be honest in all I do.

I think that I should have been a much better sociably adjusted person, and more capable at practical things if I'd not been forced to attend school where the English teacher once thrashed me black and blue because the girl behind me spoke uninvited in class and she thought it was me. She was entitled to thrash me with a cane, shredded at the end to make a whip, just as the maths master was entitled to order me to spend the entire lesson in the corridor and the needle-work teacher was entitled to pull me in front of the girls and ostentatiously trim my nails for me, while telling the other girls about me being a disgrace to girlhood. After all, they were professionals beings made to breath the same air as one of the great un-washed.

I never did say – "Where did I come from, mummy?" I felt, well I was here, now, so would make what I could of it, so I just tried to blend in somehow until I came to the conclusion, Glory Be, there could be one person who would always respect me, and sod anybody who did not want to know that I deserved to.

Some of the teachers were nice people and I'm sorry I was not a bit more appreciative.

So, that's who I was, introspective, quiet and cynical with no respect for any authority and no faith in anything. So, imagine my grateful astonishment on reading the New Testament and finding myself introduced to a man who was Sincere, Kind, Brave, Honest, Wise and aware of what he was talking about, of course he was nothing but dust by now, but once upon a time such a person had existed and his teaching had survived.

With my poor education I had no way of knowing that he was not the only one so I was inspired, exalted, at having found a Hero to Live by, and I made up my mind that as he advocated the straight and narrow path, that was for me. I did not know that this path was all right for Heroes who could tread it with ease and courage and confidence, and all right for Saints who had a staff of faith for support along the rough bits, but what did I have, as a scruffy, flea-ridden, limping mongrel dog snuffling along on the scent of a long-dead master! So that is how I set out to follow the straight and narrow path, but not saying much as I did not expect to encounter other than clever-dicks out to take the rise or nice kind and introduce me into this much wanted vaunted "Real World", in which people are aware, all sophisticated, that it is, oh, terrible thing, Old Fashioned, to not appreciate that in the Real World there is not just White and Black but many decent shades of Grey, ever increasing.

It's very old fashioned indeed to have to have two eyes and one nose though it still works for most people. Perhaps one day some impressive and adored Celebrity will start a fashion for having no nose and then some beauticians will earn a fortune cutting off noses.

So there was me, this priggish dogmatic idealist starting down the spiritual path of the straight and narrow without help, or any belief in getting any, not that I had any faith that it could lead anywhere, except, possibly to disaster, but I wanted it for its own sake, at least it might not have stretches unable to be walked, except in shite up to your ankles.

My inbox old-maid type of character was balanced, however, by an enjoyment of humour, if only because the flower of humour grows out of the seed of truth, as a rule, so I got on with people all right, if they enjoyed a laugh. This was a family trait.

I can't resist telling you this – When the king died, to leave the throne to Elizabeth II my mother and a girl next door talked about it over the fence and Margery said, most dramatically, "Mrs Pigwam, Mrs Pigwam, it don't matter how big you are, when your time is up you will still die. Mrs Pigwam, if when it's your time to die, even if your arse is dripping with diamonds, you will die just the same." My mother said Po-faced, "Will you promise me something, Marge?" "What is it?" asked Marge. "Well," said mother, "if my arse does happen to be dripping with diamonds as I die, would you please, pick them off. I would hate them to be wasted."

I have a head full of ironic jokes which I laugh at again and again and I share them with anyone who is willing to listen. I also have a heart sick with dismay at all the injustice and suffering in this world, but I keep quiet about it as most people have enough to worry about. So, this is who is writing this book. "Laugh and the world laughs with you, weep, and you weep alone. The poor old earth must borrow it's mirth but has trouble enough of its own."

To proceed – Jesus said "*and the Lord commended the unjust steward in that he had done wisely for the children of this world are wiser in their own generation than the children of light.*" But, the children of this world are now in a generation of starting to look at where being wiser than the children of light has got us and there is growing a longing for starting again.

2

I now tell the story of my life pointing to jig-saw bits as they occur. My mother got what she could out of her life, day by day as it happened along, and though she had inherited a bit of a witchy gene she never thought about it and only used it matter of factly if she had a real need, and she seemed to have no sense of wonder about it in any way.

Once she told me in course of conversation, in a disinterested sort of way that when I was a baby the doctor said that I was now too ill to survive, and she really must get some sleep. "Tonight, little mother, sleep, for your own sake and for the sake of your other children who need you. First, get the parson to come here and baptise her so that she might be buried as a Christian, then, get some sleep, and get someone in to watch her while you rest."

Mother sent for the parson and collapsed into an exhausted sleep, and she asked her mother to watch me that night. This is why I was the only sister without a 2nd Christian name, and to not be baptised in a church as I was expected to die. At 94 I am still here!

"Then," said mother "I was in a lovely sleep and mother shook me awake."

She hollered out – "I'm not going to tell anyone what I saw this night and I'm never coming in this house again. The baby will not die."

And she hurried off. Mother recited this in a bored sort of 'yer, you live in a queer things' sort of way – years later I wished I had asked some questions, but it was too late then.

The old woman knew some Gipsy spells, she was good at reading the cards, and she charmed away warts. Did she do something? Or did she nod off and have a nightmare? I'll never know now. When I was three years old mother used to take me downstairs with her early in the morning –

Comfy chair, cheerful little fire, soft light from small oil lamp, silence of 1924 early morning. Although my infant brain did not know, something in my soul knew that this was complete peace, rare and precious and I looked gratefully towards mother. She had been replaced by another woman, an ordinary woman, but, a stranger. She spoke to me in a silent voice, her aspect of one who delivers a message of which she felt no personal involvement – thus – "Century after century you have been worked upon and you have always failed. This is your last time here and if it sees your final failure the consequences will be unendurable though you will have to endure them. Intercession has been made for you but the law cannot be changed, but you may choose, if you wish, to not take the final test, and incarcerate into one of these instants of the peace you have learned to so value, for eternity, instead."

I screamed, though as silent as she – "Like a living fly encased in Amber? No, no, no."

"Careful," she said, think, consider the cost, the awful cost, of a final failure."

I howled silently, "I won't fail, I won't, let me try."

With that she turned back into my mother, I remembered. At intervals I wondered how I could possibly remember something which could not possibly have happened but I considered that it was all too daft to bother about, for one thing, how could I be expected to succeed at something I knew nothing about? Hooey, Tooey, Phooey.

But could this have been a part of the jig-saw? There is such a thing as re-incarnation and a purpose in it? I don't know.

When I was sixteen I cycled to work with a girl new to me, then, (SNOBBY) little village and her mother turned out to be a medium who told me things I did not believe, but which turned out to be true, as told to her about some dead relatives of mine from the spirit world. Could this be another piece of the jig-saw? There are other dimensions you Wot Not of? The medium spoke to me again – "I have been asked to tell you that you have been appointed a guide to whom you should listen, who will tell you so in connection with flowers.

I was talking to Anne, the medium's daughter, and she said, "I'm going to a spiritualist meeting at the Cherry tree now, you can come if you like." It turned out to be psychometry, you put your article in one of the small compartments of a box and one by one the medium holds the article and tells of any impressions. Caught on the hop I only had, to put in, a small Posy of artificial flowers which I took off my coat collar.

The medium said to me "I can't read these flowers but I am told to say to you – you have been appointed a guide and you should listen to her. I didn't think so, I felt I'd always had enough people around, expecting me to listen to them and never willing to listen back, and I didn't even know who or what this one was. However she came to win my belief and my admiration. We do have a guardian Angel.

Later, another medium said to me – "Your guide wants to tell you that she cannot give you a baptisonal name, but if you wish to use a name for her, you may call her Grace. The penny did not drop. She might as well have said "Call me Edna." I would like to say here that I can't keep looking back to see if I am repeating myself, so if I do this I will need to be excused on the grounds that I am very old and it's what old people do.

I did do a test on this guide and I 'said' to her "Imprisoned as I am in my little head I have just a narrow perspective of what I am like. How do you see me?" A silent voice 'said' to me "I see you as like a valuable article of furniture, blighted by Blue Bloom and my agenda is to restore you back to what you were designed to be."

I decided that if I shortly found out somehow that Blue Bloom on furniture could be eradicated I would take it that I had been 'spoken' to.

Shortly after this my sister Kit, (I was convinced that such a good person as Kit did not deserve to have to live in a world like this) as often, gave me some copies of Women's magazines, as I never bought any. On the second page of the first one I opened it said - HOUSEHOLD HINTS'- it said, 'IF YOU HAVE A GOOD ARTICLE OF FURNITURE WHICH IS INFECTED WITH BLUE BLOOM, THIS IS HOW TO RESTORE IT' – Well, this was more than 70 years ago, so all I remember as to this is that you finish off with a rub with a very soft cloth. I was surprised by the idea that Blue Bloom could be eradicated. Not that I was ever going to own any quality stuff or need to know how to restore any. But I had been 'spoken' to rather convincingly. Something was trying hard to make me listen, so hard and consistently that there was nothing else for it but to take it seriously.

Jesus said "*He will give his Angels charge over you.*" One week, before the 2nd World War became nearer, my mother had no money to pay the rent, a very frightening thing in our non-welfare age, but she was not frightened. She confidently walked the street, chanting again and again "Somehow or other the Lord will provide," and she was not surprised to eventually see lying in the ground, a gold coin (I can't spell its name, worth one pound, enough to pay the rent for more than one week in those frugal days). This was the world she lived in and she had nothing against it. Sometime after the war she got upset about her favourite son-in-law not paying her his usual Saturday visit. Then she drank a cup of tea, swirled the dregs round and said to me "Read this, and tell me why Jim didn't come today."

"I don't read tea leaves," I pleaded, "I don't know how to."

"Just say what shape the leaves look like," she ordered.

"Well," I said, "It's a shape like an Elephant's bottom with a wheel instead of a tail."

"Now say what that means," she insisted, so I had a little think, and, not believing in any of it, but just to appease her, I said "Well, suppose we call an Elephant's bottom a big end, and suppose we say that the wheel represents a car, then there is something wrong with the big end of Jim's car and that is why he could not drive to here.

The next Saturday Jim turned up, to my bewilderment, saying, "Sorry I couldn't come last week mum, but the big-end of my car went."

To my further bewilderment mother said, entirely matter-of-fact, "Yes, I know, Vi told me all about it!" But, that was her.

Another time I brought home six miniature roses and I put them in small pots in a row in front of the window. Mother lifted out of the debris a cotton thin rotten stem with a tiny dead leaf hanging on, saying "What about this one."

"That won't grow," I told her.

"Yes it will," she insisted, "put it with the others." Anything for a quiet life, I did so and every day she looked at the 7th pot and knew that a rose would appear. I looked too, and knew that of course it would not. However, an elder sister asked me to help sort her London flat, as she was moving home. Two days later I got back and saw three tiny green specks atop the 7th pot, which soon grew into a brighter little rose than any of the others. I don't know why I felt no surprise. But that was her.

Things which by the laws of rational thinking and common-sense could not happen, kept on happening as if this Angel appointed to me was saying to me "There is another reality behind the one which is seen by the human brain and I shall keep on saying so in any way I can until you either accept it or else ask me to leave you, which request from any person, must be obeyed in accord with the principle that free-will, whatever form it takes, must always be allowed, as it is the true expression of who you really are. But, do not deliberately reject or ignore we who want to help you and we will not get tired of trying to help for as long as you live and don't go."

3

GOD HAPPENINGS

I worked in a works canteen and one day, the men sitting at long tables, I went round collecting used plates, one of them said to me "Put the Pharaoh in the little plastic coffin." It seemed to be a harmless if silly request, so I did it and the Pharaoh, as I fully expected, laid quiet in the coffin. The men gaped at the coffin, gaped at me, gaped at each other!

"What?" I asked.

Nobody spoke, but a few days later I learned that the Pharaoh and coffin could be bought in a joke shop the joke being the look of surprise on the face of anyone who tried to put the Pharaoh in the coffin, only to see it whiyy straight up in the air and fall down beside it. No-one could make the Pharaoh lie still but I had expected him to, and he did. You would think they would ask me to do it again, but some people cannot be surprised without also getting disconcerted.

Once, I said to the canteen manager "I dreamed last night that you told me that you would have left this job by Christmas." He said, "So it's true, that there's something a bit weird about you. I will be gone by Christmas, I've got a better job."

But this is what struck me; he would not have told me if I had not first dreamed that he had done so. I once dreamed that I stood by the machines at work, nearest to the gangway, when a dear little, humorous, one of the male workers, came and stood by me and we exchanged a smile and hello. Next day I was put to run those particular machines and he came up to me and said "I dreamed last night, Vi, that you and I stood looking at each other by these very machines." I was struck by this, but I was never very good at ceasing social opportunities so I just said “Was I wearing pyjamas, or overalls.” He Said, “I didn’t notice.” Pity, it would have been interesting to know that.

Once I sat in my sister’s house and an invisible cat sat on my lap purring like mad. Half an hour later a real little tabby from next door walked in, jumped straight into my lap and purred blissfully. I noticed that if my consciousness time jumped, there was always some emotional jerking about it, as if I ‘remembered’ a few minutes of future, or more, in the way emotional impact makes past memories hit us. I loved cats and felt so pleased that the little cat fancied me that I ‘remembered’ the pleasure before it happened.

Once, I was standing in line to clock off when I heard a voice say “The pope has been shot,” I was shocked. Nobody seemed interested, so I hurried home to catch the news. There was nothing on the world news.

On the same time and day of the next week this voice said, again, exactly the same way “The pope has been shot,” and I said to the girl next to me, “Is it some joke which is going around?”

“What do you mean,” she said.

“This saying ‘the pope has been shot’,” I said.

“What makes you say that?” she said, “I only heard it said the once.”

“Oh, my brain sometimes jumps a little bit into the future,” I said, “and then when I catch up it’s as if it has happened twice, like a joke being repeated.”

She was friendly and unsurprised, “yes,” she said, “it can be like that.”

I went into an off-licence one evening and a large Alsation dog was sitting as usual in front of the counter but on this evening it did not, as usual ignore me. It looked into my face to solicit my sympathy and it stated, telepathically, “I haven’t got enough friends.” I was surprised enough to make a fool of myself, I said impulsively to the man behind the counter “Why did your dog just say 'I haven't got enough friends'?" He showed no surprise. He said, "He isn't my dog. He belongs to the people who own this place and today they went off for a jaunt without him, and he has been sulking all day."

There seems to be quite a number of people who, like my mother, feel as if this is a queer world in which you might as well expect queer incidents. Perhaps it's my capacity for being able to feel surprise is freakish?

One day my little brother came to me, trembling, and told me that his teacher had told the class that the scientists were making an experiment which could soon result in the end of the world (splitting the atom). My feeling was that the callous, arrogant bastards probably were willing to treat the world as their property to gamble with and that the possibility of destroying millions of different people and creature was neither here nor there to them, and that the sheep government would rather lead them as sheep to the slaughter than exercise the authority they were well paid to do, and that the least the teacher coward, was to rather lead them as sheep to the slaughter than exercise the authority they were well paid to do, and that the least the teacher could do, the stinking coward, was to let the kids enjoy what time they had left by keeping his big mouth shut, instead of sharing his fear with little children.

As it was I needed to go against my creed and to lie to him, so I persuaded him that of course our society was not as insane as the teacher said, and that there was nothing to worry about. I really felt that part of our society's insanity was that it was wrong to put one child into unnecessary danger but all right to do so where millions could be involved, just to prove how clever you are.

Some years later I lay in bed with a bad bout of bronchitis. I was able to breathe with difficulty while awake but every time I fell asleep I stopped breathing, and I got more and more exhausted until I cried out in my mind "Help me to sleep." At once I was floating all relaxed and comfy on my back in the air. The daft thing was that I was covered with a cloth of some kind which soothed me somehow, and that I could 'see' that although there could have been no reality in it, it was about 60 inches long and 25 inches wide and with neatly bound edges. I heard a voice say "She is sleeping peacefully now," as I drifted off to sleep. When I woke up I saw two pair of hands, no bodies, which massaged me from over one shoulder to under the opposite one (I was back in bed). The owners of the hands seemed to know I had awakened for a voice said to me "We are dispersing the phlegm." A human real voice. "You can't disperse phlegm," I protested, "it has to be choked up."

"Do not interfere with the work," said the voice, a calm and impressionable sort of voice. The massage was soothing and I shut up and went to sleep. I woke next morning with my chest completely clear. I did not believe it and I kept taking deep breaths expecting to feel congestion, but no, my chest was completely clear. If you need paranormal help, try asking clearly, even if you have no faith.

One day when I thought I had a problem, I silently said to my guide "I am going to spiritualist meeting tonight, would you be there, please." As soon as I sat down the medium said to me "Your guide is here, she said you asked her to come." To my disappointment the medium gave no opinion about my problem and just said that the guide was singing a song I had never heard of "*There's a peace we can win again, and together, somehow, we will, in the land of Begin Again, on the other side of the hill.*"

Much later I realised that I did not have a problem, it was just me, as rather often, being daft, but it would have disconcerted me to be told so. Also that my guide would never hurt my little feelings as no-one benefits from being force-fed. We learn better at our own pace. I wrote a poem to preface the one book I got published starting with "*There are things words cannot teach. There are places words cannot reach,*" as at least I knew that much.

Many people think that because they can't process the fact that truth can be stranger than fiction, are of the opinion they can explain away anything with science and co-incidence, and never wonder about if there might be ass many holes in this as there is in other ideas. Strange incidents have grown rather rare in my life as old age ever robs me of various kinds of energy, but now I include myself in telling a most fairly recent one.

A woman was anxious about not having seen her cat for some days and as she had published her phone number I had phoned sympathy and a promise to keep a look out. Then I got a silly idea and I said to my long-dead, once lodger, "Jack, you were a cat lover who would always put yourself out to help a cat, or any fellow creature. Could you locate this cat and get it home?" The next day the woman was good enough to phone me saying "I feel you will be pleased to know that my cat came home last night." Co-incidence? How would I know?

One of the last occasions when I saw a medium was in a group visit to a flower medium. We all put our flowers on a table and the medium held them and gave for each a reading. She said to me "I see a fountain throwing around sparkling water and it is you, and your Karma is now clear. You are a communicator, carry on communicating." So there it apparently is – I started as one in threat re A bad Karma given to understand that I had been allocated a helping guide, given the all-clear.

4

STRANGE EXPERIENCES

Mother just would not stop crying because her dog was dead and I said to her "You did not keep crying when any human died so why can't you stop crying about the dog?"

She was astonished and indignant, she said "But that dog was more human than any human being."

Not much of a compliment for the dog, but I suppose she meant more angelic than any human, which she was.

I remembered that many years before, I had, when ready to do my night-shift at work I had played at throwing my mind out for a few minutes before leaving the house, with a request to have 'brought back' some unexpected item from the evening paper, which I read during the break. Once it gabbled out (it used to have to speak very fast as it was coming back in, or it would have lost it). Very old, made of gold, something to do with you. In the evening paper – silly story re a railway carriage in which sat a professor who had with him a parcel containing an ancient gold vase and infant who had with him a parcel containing his beloved gold-painted potty with a picture of his hero, Donald Duck, on the inside bottom. Parcels got mixed up etc. Daft. Very old made of gold that was the ancient vase of gold. Something to do with you, I was partnered at work with a woman, who whenever she got aggravated used to say "Oh piss on it, and I was trying not to form the same habit, from constantly hearing this remark, Piss on it. The infant did, on Donald Duck so I thought – Could I still do it?

And perhaps, thinking hard of the dog and asking for something comforting to purvey to mother re the dog? I found myself staring at an old tabby cat of ours who had died more than 20 years previously and she telepathically bitterly ‘said’ to me “All that fuss about that dog, I lived with you as well I liked you (liked, not loved?!) Talk about me sometimes, think about me.” Ever since I try to do so.

Not long after I heard, as I lay in bed, Sandy run in and I felt her jump on the bed, so of course, I put my hand down, to prove that this was an illusion, and I touched fur. I said to myself “Oh I know what this is. It is the sort of vivid dream where you think you are awake when really you are asleep and dreaming, so I shall keep my eyes shut so as not to wake up, and cuddle her, while the dream lasts.” After a time the dog said ‘said’ to me “Take me back to my grave.”

When I got downstairs with her, she was, I saw, now wrapped in my jacket in which I had buried her. When we got to the grave she vanished and it struck me then, how eerie this was and I got frightened and wished I was safely back in bed. At once, I was. In the morning I was thinking of what a strange dream I had last night. Shouting as if indignant “You got the dog back. I know it. I smelt her all down the stairs and out to the back door.” in rushed mother. She had a strong sense of smell and sometimes moaned about odours to which I was insensitive. Once over the shock she liked the idea of the dog being still able to visit even though invisible, she said she could sometimes still smell Sandy, so knew when she was near. I only smelt her when I used to treat the sores she broke out into. The stuff the vet gave me did not help, so I used to cut off the fur around the sores, bathe them in a weak solution of Dettol and water and finish with a little dab of Vaseline.

This healed her each time, for many months possibly she was just allergic to something. Sandy was very co-operative and stood very still and silent during this except one day when I got upset and started crying out “Oh, poor little dog, why should she have to suffer this? Such a good little dog, what did she do to deserve to put up with this?” and so on. Mother said to me “You aren’t half making her feel sorry for herself.” This made me aware that the dog was crying out with me, she had not felt hard-done-by until I showed her how.

One day my sister Kath visited from London. She paused in the hallway and said "That's funny I could swear I'm smelling your dog."

"You are, Kath, She has come to greet you," said mother. Kath had no use at all for the paranormal and she quickly changed the subject.

Another elder sister visiting said to mother "This house is haunted."

After I was living elsewhere and I visited my brother John he suddenly said to me "If this house used to be haunted it must have been you who haunted it. Nothing strange has ever happened since you left."

Perhaps I retained into my further years an adolescent proneness to Poltergeist? How should I know? At least nothing got chucked about, nothing worse than invisible feet walking about. It happened once during the night-shift at work as I sat facing the double doors with my co-worker in the canteen. We heard a man's work boots mount the steps outside, and start to walk down the corridor towards where at the end, there was a sink where he could rinse out his and his mates tea-cans, we heard them rattle and watched for him to appear as he walked past these large, open, doors. We heard him walk past them, cans still rattling but he remained invisible. I turned to Mary opening my mouth to pass a remark about it, and her eyes stuck out and her hands clawed as if she wanted to attack me. She screeched "Don't say anything, don't ever say anything." I felt frustrated but I did not dare to ever mention it to anyone. She frightened me more than he did. I was at my machine at work when I saw in front of me a screen like a television screen, and in it a picture of my home living room, there sat my mother, her friend and my brother. On both ends of the mantelpiece a lighted candle, on the hearth rug sat Sandy. Sandy leaned out of the picture and 'said' to me "It is 6 o'clock and I am with you."

"That is stupid," I thought, "I shall be working until 7pm as we have to fulfil a contract in time." Somewhere between 5 and 6 o'clock all machines stopped and the lights went out. Presently the manager came with a big torch and said "I can't find out what is causing the black-out, nor when it will end, so you might as well all go home." As this work-place was a five minute walk from my home I was indoors by 6 o'clock and all was as on the screen I had seen, except there was no dog sitting on the rug, or if there was, I could not see her.

I worked at many different jobs and one evening, on the way home from one, I passed a venue in which a spiritualist meeting was being held so I went in. The medium was a flower medium, who strangely knew no flowers by name other than roses and tulips, but he described to everyone flowers he said were brought by spirits to each one and many said thanks, like "Yes they were so and so favourite flowers, and, yes, my husband grew those, and then he described the giver whom all claimed to recognise. (They don't make any gifted mediums like they used to).

He said to me "You are being given a bunch of small daisy-like flowers with ferny-like leaves." and I recognised these as having the popular name of Dog-Daisies a favourite of mine. This medium kept looking around in a baffled sort of way. He said "I can't see who is bringing them to you." Then he cried out, as if in alarm "IT'S A DOG, A LITTLE GOLDEN DOG," and he looked shaken and he left me flat. I wished I could put to him that my guide could blend her mind in with that of the dog, so it was not really just a dog giving flowers.

I was told more than once that I could train as a medium but I felt that I did not have a suitable personality for it. Ability is not necessarily suitability, it's a pity some don't know this. I once read a suggestion that all animals are not really animals in the way they seem to be, I think that they are quite natural animals, only with an extra dimension of some sort.

One day I was walking down the street when I 'heard' the dog say something about "The blue flowers round the box," and later I was given some tiny bulbs and not knowing what else to do with them I put them round the dog's grave and when they resulted into small blue flowers I realised that the grave was square, like a box. It's been well said that "If you allow yourself the luxury of integrity, it will be the only sort that this world will allow you." Jesus said "Blessed are you when men shall revile you and persecute you and say all manner of evil falsely against you for my sake." Hear, hear, but at least you will sleep of a night.

To go on with strange incidents I woke one afternoon when on the night-shaft on a very cold winter day, my glass of water frozen solid as we had no central heating, to find the bedroom full of the flower scent of the recognised but could not name. Next morning, having while working, experienced the scent again and recognised it as the scent of roses, I was walking to the yard gates on my way home when this silent voice 'said' to me "Have you ever thought of Heaven as a large white rose?"

"Give over," I said, just as silently, "Not my style."

"Make a note," 'said' the voice.

Not long after I saw on a second-hand book stall, a book by Dante, so I bought it out of curiosity. It described various purgatory and it went on to say that in Heaven, God sat on his throne surrounded by circle of white-clad Angels so Heaven looked like a white rose. It made Heaven sound very boring.

I meant to say how I found out that mother's dog very telepathic was. Just after the 2nd World War, luxuries were hard to come by, and, unknown to me, the baker (on his rounds), they brought bread in a van, allowed my mother one little cake every day which she shared with the dog. One day the dog met me at the door with a miserable look and as I looked at her she said telepathically at once "I found out today how awful life can be. Mum did not give me any cake today, and much worse, she was not sorry for me. She does not love me anymore."

"Yes she does, sweetheart," I said, "It's just that she has no empathy. I'll tell her about it." I went into the kitchen after mother and I said "Why did you not give the puppy any cake today?"

"But how did you know about the cake?" she asked me.

"The dog told me as soon as I came in," I said. This did not strike mother in the least as strange, but she enthused, dead serious, "Oh what a wonderful little dog."

"Yes," I said, "But you did not seem to care about her disappointment, you did not give her a kiss or a sympathetic word, instead, and she thinks that this is a sign that you don't love her anymore, you have broken her little heart."

"Oh," said mother, "Oh, oh," and she whipped the dog off the floor, with cuddles and kisses and urgent declarations of love which appeased little Sandy. Now, at first glance this would probably seem to be a ridiculous tale, but I think it works like this – it is the emotional 'essence' of a situation which reaches from one mind to another and this gets interpreted into language by the brain.

One day my work mates sitting round a canteen table during break-time were telling each other which horse they were backing in next day's Derby Race. Then someone said "I wonder which one will really win, and a silence fell as they all considered."

"I was amused they don't know it," I thought. "But they are holding a séance. Surely the name of the winning horse must be floating above this table. I did not mean it or expect anything to happen, but, a hand reached out of the top of my head, groped about, pulled into my head not a horses name, not the shape of the name, but the 'essence' of the shape of the name, and left it there. Next day, Derby Day, was my day off as I worked odd shifts. My mother said to me, “I am going to ask my friend to put my bet on. Shall I ask her to put one on for you?”

I said, “No I have no money.”

“I’ll lend you sixpence,” said mother (shows how long ago that was) it’s alright.”

I said, “Hand me ‘The Mirror’. I don’t have the slightest idea of how I did this but I went down the list of horse names and compared the ‘essence’ of shape of the names with the ‘essence’ of the essence shape in my head until I found a match and I backed that. It came in first and mother got angry.

“Why didn’t you tell me that you knew the name of the winner?” She snapped, “I would have put the rent money on it.” Well for one thing, I never believed it would come in first, and for another, I would not try to get anything at all by occult means. Those who do, are made to eventually pay for it more than it is worth. DON’T DO THIS EVER.

To be continued in Book Two.

Jig-Saw Pieces

BOOK TWO

By

Violet Pilgrim

1

I do not at all fancy myself as a Guru, though I believe I was naturally equipped to put on a good show as such, and to make profit from credulous people of whom this world is well furnished, but I didn't want to.

Now, about fellow creatures, I don't know if I am only saying what has been better said before, but I have observed this – most and possibly all are telepathic, but in some this gift is nearer to the surface of the mind, than with some others, with whom what seems to them to be in some way urgent, jolts it into use.

My whitely cat, Kate, could give out telepathy but whether she could receive it I never knew.

LONG STORY

Bob could both give out and receive. A previous cat, called Bingo received remarkably well, I said to him one day "I get the impression, Bingo, that you more or less understand, well, human language, and I want to try put a little test. Now Bingo, there is a chair near the window and I ask you to sit upon it." Bingo went straight to the chair, patted the leg of it three times and turned upon me an enquiring face of 'Have I done alright?'

Although I do have empathy I have weak and almost non-existent telepathy, but it could be connected into that of a creature of greater gift if shaken up. With the cats, of all the oddball intelligence of this species, Bingo was the most gifted. But of course I did not get long to really get to know him and what he could do.

"Break, break, break, on thy cold grey stones, oh sea. And I would that my tongue could utter the thoughts that arise in me." When I first was taking refuge from spite endured in my home town, by living in Walton, this sweet

and amiable place, I discovered that behind the back fence which was something like two feet above the ground behind it, among the thick Hawthorn trees there lived a colony of assorted stray cats. They lived on anything they could find to eat. I would not be able to tell the sex of a cat if I studied one on my lap but what little I saw of them, I seemed to see that there were two females, firm friends to each other, and perhaps five males. They obviously felt that they could manage without humans.

But one day, and I am not necessarily expecting to be believed here, I was working at the bottom of the garden, when a half-grown cat, a tortoiseshell, as beautiful in shades of black, grey, white, ginger and apricot, as if painted by an artist came through the fence and stood before me and 'said' (I'm sorry but she **did**) "I think that my life is going to be very hard and I need a human to stand by me for if I ever need such help. I think you could be such and in return I will obey you." It was as if she had studied humanity.

I said, "Sit down." She sat. I said, "Stand." She stood. "Go," I said. She started off apparently satisfied that she had tried her best. Just as she was going to slip through the fence I said, "Come back." She came back. She looked at me as if to say, "Now you know." This is making me feel a fool. But "Tell the truth and shame the Devil." I saw nothing more of her until there came such a cold winter that prey must have been scarce, and the cats got very hungry.

Late one afternoon as I looked out prior to locking the back door, like I always did, as I gave a final look round a multi-coloured small head poked out from the gap between the shed and the side fence. "Oh, are you hungry?" I asked. She came out and a line of assorted cats came out behind her and there they stood in a row. "Sit down," I said to the leader. She sat down, she looked along the row as if to convey "She says we must sit down." They all sat down although the tortoiseshell's best friend, a queer-looking cat, short-haired on the front half and long-haired on the back half, shot me an evil look and sat down last. I found an old tin tray and filled it up with anything I had which a cat might eat and they all gathered round and ate to the last crumb, very polite and nice. There was no pushing. Each cat ate anything which happened to be before it and when there was nothing left they filed down the garden and got through the back fence.

They must have had some source of water as I did not think of that, though I daresay the tortoiseshell would be able to let me know if they had not. Some weeks later at 2a.m. a cat was crying out at the back door. "That can't be her," I thought, but it was. So I put a saucer of food before her. She stepped aside then and an old, lame cat came out of a shadow and ate it. This was a Queen cat who looked after her people. Some weeks after, I knew that she was soon to give birth but the weather was warm and mild so I trusted her to find a hollow where she could birth her kittens in peace. But **all** that night it came on to rain as never in my life I experienced, before or since. I was worried but what could I do? Nothing. In the morning the garden was a lake and the cat lay against my back step soaked through but making no attempt to lick herself dry. She just lay there, her eyes pits of utter misery and despair as she must have been peacefully giving birth, when down came the deluge and the kittens drowned. I hunkered down beside her I let her know I was grieving with her for a time and I slowly changed my tone to one of hope and I told her "It won't always be like this, you are not alone, you have got me, I care, I will always be here for you, I am sorry for you, I care, I will always care. I will do anything to help you. I care."

Gradually a little gleam of hesitant encouragement came into her despairing eyes. She knew that she had someone to turn to, who would help to bear her burdens. She understood. Oh God, how she did. As from then, every kitten, dozens of them appeared in my front room. It was just like when men can 'poodle' off, having made a girl pregnant and leave it to the welfare state to pay the bills. But my guide saw all this. She got Jack to lead me into a charity shop, and he picked up an ornament in the shape of a ct. "Look Vi," he said.

"Oh don't," I said, "I am up to my eyeballs in cats."

The woman behind the counter came forward. "I think I can help you," she said. She introduced me to a very nice lady who had a little charity cat shelter and as long as I was willing to house each batch until weaned, she found homes for them all. "Don't worry Vi," she said, "the mature cats are hard to home, but kittens go like hot cakes."

Several months of trying to get hold of tortoiseshell puss for neutering she found out what I already knew, that this was not just a cat but a reincarnation of Houdini, famous escapologist. At long last and the end of a war which the cat kept winning, she was neutered and the flow of kittens was dried up at last. It was up to Jack, swarms of assorted cats, all bored and spoiled rotten would have stayed with us until they died. Even so, I had so many cats and I loved each one as if it was the only one. I still do and I would write a quirky one I was watching one of these game shows where the compere asks the players personal questions about their lives and she said "and do you have cats in substitute to children?" "No," said the woman, "in preference to children." I don't suppose she would have dared to say why. The woman who rescued stray cats and found homes for kittens once remarked to me that she liked cats better than humans because she knew what humans were capable of and without any provocation at that.

The tortoiseshell came to me once more, she silently informed me that she had now lost all her tribe, I understood that much, but not what fate had suddenly befallen them I don't know if she knew. She was very obviously heart-broken, and she moved in with me, as I was better than living with nobody, I suppose. She was a very clean and polite and ever anxious to please, guest. I said to her once "You are not a real cat. If you were a real cat you would sit on my lap." This most telepathic creature got on my lap and squatted there, very uneasy for about a minute. Then her nerve broke, and she sprang up and hid up. But she wanted to please and made herself do it again. Eventually she got to like it, the odd thing was that she never did treat me to a dead mouse or like that, as if she read my mind and knew that it would not please me. Did she? I don't know.

2

With regard to these invisible walkers who once in a while would be heard, well, I used to get home from the work 2-10pm shift at 10.30pm, sit with a cup of tea and a sandwich to 11pm, get up then, go into the kitchen and tweak all four gas taps to make quite sure they were off, and get to bed. One night I got in late, at 10.45pm, so I sat down for my ½ hour supper break, not at 10.30pm but at 10.45pm, these invisible feet walked across the floor – drag – plop, drag – plop, drag – plop. I thought to myself

"Well this is a turn-up for the book, I recognise that walk, I wonder whose ghost this is, come to visit me?" As I thought this, then the feet walked through the kitchen door and I heard – tweak, tweak, tweak, tweak, four gas taps (metal ones) getting tweaked and I knew that it was my own ghost. What I had never noticed before was that I walked with a drag – plop, nor had I realised until then that the gas-taps, when tweaked made a slight squeak sound (being made of metal). When I was working day-shift hours I sometimes sat in the railway station waiting for the train with three old women and on a couple of occasions I remarked that my cats would not like the heavy rain.

One morning as I walked to the station a silent voice said "Those old women are sitting there taking the rise out of you." I just sat in silence and one of them looked at me, and then they looked at each other. Having been warned I was ready. Usually when someone is ill-mannered to me I am not ready, I am baffled into silence at the way some people can lower themselves to be rude with no provocation.

One of them said to me, "It's raining," and when I just said, "Yes," she rushed into speech-thus with a mocking grin, "Yes, we know, dear, your dear little pussycats don't like nasty rain do they dear," I looked down my nose, "As a matter of fact I had no intention of saying anything about cats," and I allowed my tone of voice to say, "You nasty old Piss-takers." It was their turn to be disconcerted into silence, I felt like adding: '*When shall you three meet again? In thunder, lightning or in rain.*' But I thought they would not recognise Shakespeare, and his three witches.

A woman I know who understands a lot of eclectic stuff that's beyond my own understanding, told me that some sort of a 'thingy-what's it' travels around the universe completely visitatorial everywhere, every so many thousand years, once again and changes where it touches, has recently been to us, and I think she has something, as I have been noticing with great surprise that the humbug with which this world normally functions seems to be slowly draining away.

Only yesterday I put on the television in time to hear someone saying "All this used to be swept under the carpet." I know about the facility of our movers and shakers for sweeping stuff under the carpet. There seems as if the 'still small voice of God'; has got a bit more audible with a few more people, and the special-pleading voice is a bit more faint.

The more I've looked at this world the more I know that the reality of it is much too complicated for a literal mind like mine to expand into an understanding of it. I can only be honest about what my own bit of it is said to me, and all I know is that there was too much coincidence in it to reasonably be explained away as coincidence, and if I cannot ensure that I know much about what is going on behind and unseen by the human mind as reality I do know something is, and to sum up what it pictures after joining up the dots the **picture** is this. Ultimate reality is beyond the understanding of the human mind in its present state of evolution.

For instance I woke one morning to find that a five foot high, snow-white cat standing upright on its hind-legs was regarding me. As it blinked out of existence I 'knew' that a part of my brain must have been still asleep and dreaming for a little while. But was it entirely that? Because not long after that I read in a book that some people believe that cats are descended from some sort of ancient civilisation and that they have a God of their own, who is one of many Gods and who manifests in the shape of a giant snow-white cat. So, was this really a coincide dream, or a dip into some other dimension of reality?

I had already suspected that the human mind was constructed to walk in a straight line of time like a horse walking in a straight line wearing blinkers, to stop it from being distracted by any side view, and to have them removed at the end of that day's work? I don't know. If my experience of life with my able teach-quille in the infant class was trying to tell me anything it appeared to be this – These evangelists are right. We are not risen monkeys, we are fallen angles. We are born here as what we are, full of imperfection. We do have a guardian Angel whose job is to restore us back into spiritual wholeness.

Because our restoration should be a **real** thing, nothing against our own free-will is permitted to this Angel as the use of free-will expresses what we are. But they will use all of their limited power to help us in any possible-to-them in their DIFFERENT sort of power, if we can believe, accept, and co-operate at least, they can do things we can't. To be unable to accept this is not held against anybody but, to accept and turn your back **is** held against you. It is a rejection of the Holy Ghost and if you reject it and what it says to you and prefer the rewards of this that is down to you. I'm that case, '*you pays your penny and you takes your choice and you are stuck with what you bought*'.

'*So many beliefs so many creeds so many paths that wind and wind. And all this sad world really needs is just the art of being kind.*'

To be kind to the rest of creation is to be Honest, Compassionate, Patient and Willing-to-know, and this is the hard bit, Brave.

Well, they are all hard bits, but that is the point of your Guardian ~Angel, ready and able to do whatever is need in your particular place in your particular dimension in the universe as best it can. If like me, you can't rustle up much faith, don't worry, to do your very best to be kind, that is faith in action, just the same.

But to get back to the theme of something starting to change in this world, for instance – Jesus said *"There is nothing hidden but shall be revealed,"* and skeletons are now apt to zone out of cupboards in a manner unknown in my heyday, even in the case of someone as low-down and vulnerable as myself. I was tried and sentenced in a 'kangaroo' court many years ago and denied a chance to fight my case because I was not allowed to know what I was supposed to have done. A person with some undeserved Authority to really hurt me discussed me with my detractors and refused to discuss anything with me with a strong implication that what I might say would be a lie.

Recently, 25 years later, I had a strange dream in which a black African I could see clearly and hear distinctly said to me, "There is something in your record which you may want to have cleared up?" It did not mean anything to me I had long since stopped, felt. I know that as I was not perfect I had not earned a perfect life and brooding about it was not my favourite hobby. But I woke up a couple of mornings later with the realisation that as I slept my consciousness had done something I had not asked it to, and it had picked up on a previously missed cue which made all in connection with my ordeal, re the 'kangaroo' court, understandable to me. After 25 years?

So there it is, even the record of someone as marginalised as me had been looked at and a flaw in it explained to me. The Humbug is draining out of our world. It's just a thought but could it be that humanity is being stripped bare ready for a closer examination in a higher court? I don't know.

3

My mother was at death's door and she said to me, "Go and get the parson to come to me."

I said, "I am not going to leave you alone and I cannot get someone in at this time of night." But, Jesus said, "*If two or three of you are gathered together in my name, there I will be in the midst of you.*"

"Well, mother there are two of us so if we say a prayer, and sing a hymn with the faith that this is true, we do not need a parson."

Mother sang the hymn in a loud voice, but she stopped in the middle of it and she said in an amazed sort of way, "Violet, I can see all my dead friends and neighbours, they are all smiling and waving at me." Then she said, "Oh Vi, I can see my Kit."

"Your sister Kit?" I asked.

"No, no," she said, "My Kit." (My sister Kit who died as young as 50). Mother then burst out laughing, "Oh dear," she said, "Kit always was a funny girl and she is still the same."

"What did she say to make you laugh like that?" I asked.

There was a pause and she said in a bewildered sort of way, "Violet, I can't tell you, when I am with you I lose them, and when I am with them I lose you."

This morning after her death I was clearing up in the living room and I was saying to myself, "They are not going to push what happened to her in the hospital under the carpet if I can stop them. Hell or high water, I will get some publicity or die trying." Then I heard her voice, her audible human voice although faint and strained, she said, "Violet I don't want you to." This came as a surprise and a disappointment as she had expressed a desire for justice before her death, although I don't think that I ought to put the words in which she expressed herself in writing. Even in the vulgar world of today.

My world, of my day, was a world in which the difference between truth and Special Pleading was not as well-known even as it is now, and I knew that I never had any effective weapons with which to fight my corner, not even that powerful weapon, faith, allowed even to the disadvantaged honest dwellers in a dishonest world. I never had any faith, only a sense of justice which is not enough for a poverty-stricken female in a man's world.

Fortunately for me, I did have one advantage, as that derided character, the Old-Maid type, so I was free to do my best without worrying that you owe more to your children than you do to your principles. I am not a church goer, so I might be wrong to feel that it is not going to be mentioned in 'must have bums on seats' churches that the need to defend your children can make it hard and painful to be as straight as you would like, was mentioned by Jesus. So it was easy for me to stand up in the face of opposition where I knew I could not win as a lone female.

For instance I was once unable to earn the bonus which I depended upon because the man whose job it was to fetch me my material for working refused to serve me, and when I complained to the supervisor about it, he just laughed and said "Oh you can easily get round him, just use your feminine charm." I could have done this; I was nice-looking and naturally very articulate. But, inherently full of stiff-necked pride, I could not take the advice of Jesus about being willing to ever get down on my knees and wash anybody's grubby feet in any way. The best I could manage was to keep my big mouth shut as far as it was practical to do so.

Jesus said when he sent his followers out into the world "*I send you out as doves among snakes, be you therefore as gentle as doves and as wise as serpents.*" I always, unless a principle was involved, managed to be a gentle dove, but I was no good at being as wise as a serpent. It made me seem daft. When I got really old and looked back I could see my many, many, mistakes. You need to be either a serpent, or, a dove who is as wise as a serpent, as many people just naturally are without having to think about it, mostly, to get by.

As I think I've already mentioned, I prefaced the book I got published with a poem starting with:

"There are things which words cannot teach,
there are places which words cannot reach."

But as near as I can use words, during the course of as long life I seemed to see this – We are not risen monkeys. There are other dimensions where we shall see what, and where, we unknowingly were. You do have a gifted guardian angel but you only get what is possible if you accept and co-operate. There are evil forces which will bribe, mislead or frighten you, as possible, to keep you and your guardian apart, and you should resist them. If you are unable to have faith as generally posited. This will serve – to be honest – as harmless, and patient as you can manage and to tell your Angel how you feel even if you cannot believe he/she/it exists. You might win the jack-pot. You will be credited with faith, I tried to keep any reference to myself out of this book, but found I could not talk straight without it. To some, anything I have written about things will be old news and to others I will be a fool who could be put right by a competent psychiatrist. But there it is, I have learnt lessons and I have got too old and decrepit to having any desire to look big.

To get back to the story of my mother. Shortly after the funeral my mother's favourite son-in-law Jim, and his wife, my sister, called on me and said that they were on their way to a spiritualist meeting and that I could come too, if I liked, I did like, as usual, expecting not much, but the medium described my mother pretty well and said that she had to tell me that my mother was saying "Tell her this, don't carry out your intention, I do not want you to, I want you to forgive and forget. Please do, forgive and forget."

Well, the insults, the humbug, the threats, had got right up my nose and I said, "I would do, but I can't." She says, "Please, please." said the medium.

"I am unable," I said. The medium though in silence for a time and then she said "It has been decided that, to appease you, a small fraction of what you require will be yours. Make it do." I had been told that I had better give in as no way would I get my story in a newspaper and that in that unlikely event of my doing so I would come to be sorry. Well, after a long struggle I did get a little bit of my story into a national newspaper, after all, though not the worst of it.

Now, after all this time I heard someone say on the telly, this "A deal of what has, has gone on in our hospitals has been, in the past, swept under the carpet."

It seems to me that, yes, there is a change. It looks a bit to me as if the Humbug is draining out of some kind of little hole in human society, and we are being spruced up ready to meet – Who? What?

What is my positive opinion about all this? I don't know. I used to sleep on the sofa some nights in the cold old house and one morning I dreamed that a tiny man dressed all in brown was being threatened by two large thus and he was screaming. "Help, help, help." As I opened my eyes to get a clearer look at him, I woke up and there on top of the middle door crouched a little brown bird, a cat looking up either side. I stupidly got up and crept my hand up to it. It fell into my hand and I took it outside, when if flew strongly away???

One long hot summer when I lived with mother I saw near our back step a stray cat and it let me pick it up and examine it, though as the stray cats had learned that, "He who trusts in human nature leans on a broken reed." I knew it must have a desperate problem. I could find nothing wrong so I put down food which it ignored. With this I said to the cat “I don’t know what your trouble is but if you can think of some way to tell me I will do what I can. I don’t know if anyone can believe it, I only just can and I was there, but as I hung out the washing there was the cat. It sat holding the dish in which I used to put water in case some creature might need it. The cat held the dish with one paw to face the empty inside bottom to me. It was telling me that it needed water by describing a circle round and round the dry bottom!!! I think my guide kindly merged her mind into that of the cat so that it knew how to make me understand. We can do things the Angels can’t because they have to be able to utilise our physical energy since in our dimension they have none. But they can be good at this in a stronger way than most of us. So can the demons. Don’t let them in. As I said I do not fancy myself as a Guru, and I have never felt certain about much, but I wanted to talk straight as I can before I go. WHERE? I DON’T KNOW.

Last night I had a strange dream – it went like this – someone was explaining about the reality and purpose of the universe – The universe is some sort of intense Mind-Power and it has experimented widely and blindly with trying to find a positive shape in which to be and it is still trying for this, the human race being part of its attempt and all around us is the result of this, it’s shaping of the essence of its mind-power into various representations of what is another groping effort to shape its essence into a positive completion of perfection. As the shape of this essence is what we are composed of, of course its shape is real to us. But we are required to co-operate in this effort and the ‘catch 22’ is that we can only be efficient at this by being set free to use our own initiative as to how we, and **if** we do co-operate as partakers of this final perfection. This is expressed by us as ‘God’ and ‘Soul’. Does any of this make sense? I don’t know.

When I was very young I was in a group of girls and these little girls were telling each other why they loved their daddy.

I was silent until one of them said to me, "Do you love your daddy?"

I said "No," and one of the little girls, with that air of great wisdom which some little girls can put on said to me, "You would not be here if it was not for your dad,"

I replied, "That is what I most have against him." I am a coward, a pessimist, with a longing to find a deep hole and pull it in after me, putting up with this dimension because any further ones might be worse and compensating with as many laughs as I can get without ever hurting anyone for the purpose. Who am I to pontificate about the nature of the universe? From an early age I have been suspiciously made aware that Angelic influences have said to me in any way they can "Never mind, anxious soul, we recognise you, we are giving you all we can with the handicap barrier of your morose disposition. We can't wet-nurse you but we will always be for you in any way allowed to us, which is not as much as we would like to do for you. Rabbit, we will, really, bend the structure of what the human mind sees as reality in order to comfort you."

It has taken too long to relate but if you will believe me there are Angels and Demons constructed from the same Mind-Power, and it would pay us to believe it. But who am I to talk? I don't know. But I know this that in regard to the war in heaven everybody is required, some time, somewhere, and somehow to state positively which made your answer the Angels will use whatever they can to help you, even when you are in the wrong it is not held against you, they do cry if you get hurt, just the same.

I've just remembered something I meant to record this. My medium friend occasionally writes me a letter, once included in one message from my friend who died several years ago it said 'Look out for forget-me-nots, not the flowers, but mention of Forget-me-nots.' Next morning I looked up from my book just in time to see going past the window a white van, with a florist's name written big on it, FORGET-ME-NOT. Then the CLEAN-EASY woman called and she showed me some photos, one of which was of her garden and she said "Those flowers in the front are FORGET-ME-NOTS. Next evening, I was reading a magazine and found myself looking at mention of a spiritualist church which was named THE FORGET-ME-NOT CHURCH. CO-INCIDENCE? I think not, I could hundreds more incidents but I am tired.

THE END!!!

www.ingramcontent.com/pod-product-compliance
Ingram Content Group UK Ltd.
Pitfield, Milton Keynes, MK11 3LW, UK
UKHW042001190726
13854UKWH00005B/2112

9 781787 195790